The CHOSEN PROJECT

- Book One -

ENOCH'S TRUTH & EXILE

A.J. Moore

ISBN: 979-8-9933001-1-5 (paper back)

ISBN: 979-8-9933001-0-8 (Digital)

Dedication

To those who walk between stars and soil, never forgetting the weight of both.

Epigraph

"Knowledge fills the hands, but what fills the arms?"

Acknowledgment

To the ancestors who walked both paths, exile and return.

About the Author

A.J. Moore writes at the intersection of myth, memory, and legacy. Drawing inspiration from ancient narratives, human nature, and the enduring search for meaning, he crafts stories that explore exile, belonging, sacrifice, and the unseen costs of wisdom.

Introduction: Enoch and the Weight of Time

The story of Enoch has always been wrapped in mystery. In ancient texts, he was the man who "walked with God" and then was no more, vanishing from the earth without a trace. Generations wondered if he was taken, if he ascended, or if his fate was sealed beyond human knowing.

But there is another explanation, one born not of faith alone but of physics: time dilation. When one moves through the cosmos, near stars, near gravity wells, near the edges of black holes, time itself bends.

What feels like years to the traveler may pass as millennia for those left behind. For Enoch, exploration among the stars may have been his covenant and his exile at once. In chasing knowledge, he stepped into realms where clocks falter, and in doing so, he lost not only his home but his place in the human story.

This book is an account of his return. It is not triumph, not even redemption, but the search for both. It is the journey of a man who mapped constellations and coded memory into light, only to discover that wisdom carries a cost: distance. A father, a husband, a man who loved his people, was forced to confront the truth that while he studied the eternal, his family and descendants moved on without him.

Every scene you read here is his attempt to cross the gulf that time carved. Every word is his reaching hand, extended across centuries. It is Enoch's way of asking if home can still exist when time itself has become the barrier.

Opening Scene: The Atlas and the Door

The air was still, as if the cosmos had been holding its breath for centuries. Enoch stood alone in the Library of Stars. Volumes floated around him like lanterns, their spines pulsing with constellations. He opened one, the script was alive, curling into shapes of memory and song. But it was the Atlas that called him. A book bound in leather, worn by hands long before his. When he touched it, the pages unfurled into maps of time: rivers that ran backward, mountains that shifted with every heartbeat, entire eras sketched in fire and light. And there, etched into one of the maps, a sigil he knew by blood. His family crest, faint but unbroken, was carved into a land where voices sang and fires burned with joy. "Here," he whispered, as if the cosmos itself might confirm. "Here they thrive." With trembling hands, Enoch pressed the page. The map rippled like water and pulled him through.

Impact. His body slammed against soft earth, lungs filling with air that tasted like harvest. Around him, fields stretched golden and endless. Beyond them: a village alive with laughter, music, and children running in bright clothes. He rose, knees weak, eyes stinging. He knew their faces, his children's children, and those yet unborn. Generations, thriving without grief. A feast stretched across a long table, bread steaming, wine pouring, stories spilling into the dusk. He staggered forward, a smile breaking through the centuries. "Family!" His voice cracked the air like thunder. Heads turned. Silence fell. The joy drained from their faces. Where there was laughter, there was fear. A woman clutched her child closer. Men stood, wary, forming a wall between him and the table. Enoch froze, reaching out. "It's me. I've come home." The eldest among them, a man with eyes like tempered steel, shook his head.

His voice was steady, almost mournful. "You don't belong here." The words cut deeper than any blade. Before Enoch could answer, the wind shifted. A presence filled the air, vast, unseen, pressing against his bones. A voice moved through the silence, neither loud nor soft, but absolute: "You traded your place for knowledge. You chose the stars over the table. That covenant cannot be undone." Enoch dropped to his knees, the weight of eternity pressing down. For the first time since he left the earth, he wondered if wisdom had made him more or less than human.

Scene 2: The Covenant Denied

Enoch's knees dug into the soil. The words echoed in his chest, "You traded your place for knowledge…" A shudder, the harvest wind carried the scent of wildflowers and distant rain. He lifted his hands, trembling with urgency. "No. No, I chose both." His voice broke. "I studied the cosmos, yes, but my heart always beat for this place. For you." The sound of footsteps hardened on the path behind him. The woman with the child pressed the child closer. Children glanced at each other; laughter had become hushed murmurs. The eldest man, the one with eyes like tempered steel, advanced. His robe draped with badges of lineage, marked by age and ritual. He held a wooden staff carved with symbols of earth and seed. "You are beyond the covenant," he said, voice steady. "To prove yourself here, one must dwell the way we dwell: born of earth, memory unfractured by celestial rift." Enoch's palms stung. He reached for his pocket and pulled out a fragment of star-matter, a small orb glowing with constellations, particles humming with code. "I carry memory," Enoch said. "I carry things you have forgotten." A hush. Then, the man tilted his head. "They've forgotten, yes, because some knowledge dissolves memory. And in forsaking earth, you left the realm. You may walk among us. But you cannot claim what only those rooted here may pass." Enoch stood, rage and grief folding into one.

Shadows lengthened across the feast hall as elders gathered, closing the gap between him and the family. "Then I will reclaim a place," Enoch whispered. "By whatever covenant or cost." He stepped forward, and the woman with the child, protective of her own, stepped back. The child's eyes were blinking in fear. The eldest raised the staff: a shimmering line in the air – not a weapon, but a barrier of light. The warmth of the evening dimmed. The music of celebration drums, wind, and pipes faltered. "You have your answer," the eldest said. "No place here." Enoch's knees buckled. The lands he had crossed, stars he had mapped, none prepared him for this final rejection. He fell into the dirt, the fecund earth cold beneath him, the golden fields now foreign. A tear cut softly across his cheek. He looked up at the sky, silver stars winking into existence above dusk. "Then I leave," he said. "But I will not forget." And light flickered in the distance at the horizon, the atlas page shifting, the map calling once again. A new realm to seek. A new home to find.

Scene 3: The Souvenir

The horizon rippled with light, the atlas calling him toward the next realm. Enoch clenched his fist as the page began to fold around him. Wind roared, stars bent, and his body stretched thin as parchment.

Then silence. He opened his hand, expecting only the orb of starlight he had carried since the Library. It was there, pulsing faintly, but something else lay against his palm. A grain of wheat. It was so small he almost missed it, golden and warm against his skin. He turned it between his fingers. The stalk had been severed clean, as though placed deliberately. Enoch frowned. He had been barred, rejected,
cast out. Yet this fragment of their harvest had followed him. Or perhaps chosen him. The page closed behind him, and the world dissolved into darkness.

When he emerged, the air was different. Heavy, wet with salt. Waves crashed against black cliffs beneath him. A storm brewed on the horizon, lightning clawing at the clouds. This was no village of laughter and feasts. This realm was raw, unyielding, a place where survival was a daily covenant. Enoch tucked the wheat into his robe. He didn't yet understand why he kept it, only that letting go felt like tearing a thread from himself.

The cliffs were sharp, jagged like broken teeth. Wind whipped his robes as Enoch steadied himself, the sea below roaring like a creature hungry for blood. Lightning tore open the sky, briefly painting the black stone in white fire. Enoch gritted his teeth and pressed forward. His feet found a path worn into the rock not natural, but carved, as though countless others had walked this way before him. Each step echoed with a strange rhythm, like a drumbeat buried in the cliffs themselves. At the crest of the ridge, he saw them.

Figures standing against the storm. They wore cloaks of woven seagrass, their faces shadowed but their stance firm. They were not feasting. They were not laughing. They were waiting. The first raised a staff tipped with obsidian. The storm seemed to bend around him. "You are the traveler," the figure said. The voice carried in the gale, not loud, not shouting, but steady, like a current that could not be denied. Enoch hesitated, clutching the orb and the grain of wheat in his hand. "I am seeking a home." The figure stepped forward, revealing a face scarred by salt and time, eyes as deep as the sea. "There is no home in the storm," the man said. "Only trial. If you endure, you are shaped. If you falter, you are swept away." The others lifted their staffs, pounding them into the stone. The sound matched the hidden drumbeat, rolling in waves beneath the thunder. Enoch's chest tightened. He had been denied a seat at the feast.

Now he was being offered no seat at all, only a crucible. The scarred man tilted his head. "Do you still wish to walk here, exile?" Enoch looked down at his hand. The orb glowed faintly, stars within it shifting restlessly. Beside it, the grain of wheat, so small, so fragile, glimmered with its own quiet strength. He closed his hand. Raised his eyes. "Yes," he said. The storm answered with a crash of lightning so close it split the stone at his feet. But Enoch did not move. He stood, drenched, trembling, but unbroken. The scarred man's lips curled not into a smile, but something close. Respect. "Then walk," he said. "And let the storm decide if you are worthy."

The storm swallowed him, wind thrashing, waves clawing at the cliffs. Each step forward felt less like a path and more like judgment. And yet, Enoch walked. He thought of the feast of faces turned away, of a covenant denied. He thought of the stars that had whispered secrets into his bones. Knowledge had given him sight beyond sight, yet it had left him unseen by those he loved. A question rose in him, sharper than the lightning above: Was this ambition for knowledge a key to freedom? Or the bars of a prison? For the man who seeks power, the world opens wide, but it also empties, leaving him a solitary figure in the space he once called home. Enoch's grip tightened around the orb, the grain of wheat pressing against his skin. The storm raged on, but his pace did not falter. What can I possibly build that could replace what I lost?

Chapter Two–The Dream and the Waking

The storm split open, light tearing across the sky. Enoch closed his eyes and opened them again in silence. He was standing not on the cliffs, but in a garden from long ago. The air smelled of earth after rain, leaves dripping with memory.

A fire burned in the center, crackling, but it gave no heat. And across from him sat the Custodian, the one who bore neither age nor youth, who carried eternity in his gaze. "Do you remember the moment you chose?" the voice asked, neither accusing nor kind. Enoch swallowed. His hands trembled, though he felt no fear. "I remember." The fire brightened. The scene shifted. He saw himself younger, wrapped in the promise of his family's laughter, yet already restless. Above him, the stars had called, offering knowledge beyond the soil, beyond the feast, beyond even love. "You chose the sky," the Custodian said. "And the sky is endless." Enoch watched his younger self stretch out his hand, accepting the orb of starlight. The moment of covenant. The moment the fracture began.

The fire roared, then collapsed into darkness. He woke up gasping. The storm cliffs were gone. Instead, he lay in a chamber carved into the rock, warmed by a small fire, dry robes laid beside him. He rose slowly, shoulders aching, hand still clenched around the orb and the wheat. Both remained. The chamber was simple but well-provisioned: bowls of food, a jug of water, even a pile of coins stacked neatly on the stone shelf. He smiled, a bitter twist on his lips. Always, the world provides me with what I need. Money, food, shelter… Enoch was nothing if not resourceful.

He could assess a market at a glance, bargain with rulers, and gather comforts wherever he walked. These things bent easily to him. Survival was never the question. But as the firelight flickered, his eyes caught the shadows cast on the wall. Shadows that looked like children dancing. Shadows that looked like his family. The smile faded. His hand tightened. And yet what do I do? he thought. Every time I touch joy, I break it.

Every time a bond begins to form, I remember their rejection, and I destroy it before it can destroy me. He pressed the grain of wheat to his chest. It burned colder than the coin beside it. "Knowledge filled my hands," he whispered, "but emptied my arms." The fire popped, scattering sparks across the chamber. Enoch sat alone. Again. By his own design.

Enoch stirred in the stone chamber, the fire crackling low. The storm still rumbled outside, distant but steady, like the growl of a great beast pacing. He shifted upright, hand still clenched around the orb. It pulsed faintly, rhythm matching his heartbeat. He exhaled, and the light steadied, as if it were breathing with him. The chamber door scraped open. The scarred man from the cliff entered, his staff lowered but his eyes sharp. Another figure followed, younger, quiet, carrying a bundle of dried reeds. The elder's gaze fell to the orb in Enoch's hand. "What is it you clutch, exile?" Enoch's lips curled. "Memory." The man stepped forward, extending his hand. "Then share it,"

Enoch said, "nothing", simply extended his palm. The orb lay there, glowing. The elder reached out, fingers brushing against its surface, and instantly, the light died.

The orb became no more than smooth stone, cold and dull. The younger man gasped, stepping back. The elder frowned, gripping it harder, trying to coax life from its shell. Nothing.
Enoch closed his hand around it again. At once, the light bloomed back, constellations swirling inside, starlight spilling through his fingers. He looked up at them both. His voice was low, edged with quiet finality. "It only knows me."

The elder withdrew, suspicion shadowing his face. The younger man, though, leaned forward, eyes wide, not with fear, but awe.

The elder turned away, muttering something under his breath, and left the chamber with his staff tapping against the stone. The storm's echo swallowed him. The younger man lingered. His eyes stayed on the orb, then shifted to Enoch. "You… you command the light," he said softly. His voice was unsteady, not yet hardened by years. "I have never seen such power." Enoch studied him. The boy's hands were calloused, his tunic patched, his shoulders narrow but tense with hunger for more than survival. "What is your name?" Enoch asked. "Kael," the boy answered. He hesitated, then stepped closer. "Tell me… what is it? That stone. How does it know you?" Enoch opened his hand again. The orb pulsed in rhythm with his heart. "It is not stone," he said. "It is a covenant. One made long before you were born. One I paid for." Kael's brow furrowed. "Paid? With what?" Enoch's eyes darkened. For a long moment, he said nothing. The fire cracked, shadows leaping across the walls like dancers. Finally, his voice came low, almost a confession. "With what I loved most. With what I thought I could never lose." Kael sat across from him, silent.

He did not understand, not yet, but his curiosity was unyielding. "Will you teach me?" the boy asked at last. "If it only knows you… Then perhaps it can show me something through you." Enoch looked at him, really looked. A boy eager, unscarred by rejection, believing that knowledge was only a gift and never a burden. He felt the ache rise in his chest, recalling the laughter and faces turned away. He wanted to say no. To push Kael aside before the bond formed, to spare himself the pain he knew would come. But the boy's eyes were steady. They saw wonder, not exile. Enoch sighed. "Very well," he said. "Sit close to the fire. If you wish to learn, then you must first learn how to listen." Kael's face lit, and he shifted nearer, knees brushing the stone. The orb glowed brighter, casting constellations against the chamber walls. Enoch lifted it, letting the stars dance across Kael's wide eyes. And though his heart was clenched with old wounds, for the first time in countless ages, he spoke not to himself but to another. "Let me tell you," He said, "how the sky first called my name."

The storm eased to a restless drizzle by morning. Enoch and Kael emerged from the stone chamber into the grey light. The sea frothed below the cliffs, still angry, but the air carried a fragile calm. Kael walked ahead, proud of his new connection to the traveler, orb-light still dancing in his mind. But the village boys waited on the path, older and broader, their faces sharp with mischief. "Kael," one sneered. "You've found yourself a father, eh? Or is he just another mouth for you to follow?" The others laughed. One stepped forward and shoved Kael hard in the chest. He stumbled, fists clenching. His face burned. Enoch watched silently. Kael turned to him, desperate. "They mock me. They think I am nothing. What should I do?" Enoch's voice was calm.

"What do you want to do?" Kael's fists shook. "Strike him. Show them I am not weak." Enoch nodded slowly. He reached into his robe and drew the orb. Its light flickered, casting long shadows across the boys' faces. "Violence is a response," Enoch said, his voice low, steady. "It is quick, sharp, and it ends as soon as the blow lands. But true power" He lifted the orb, and the glow expanded, wrapping their path in light. "True power bends the world without striking it." The bully scoffed, stepping closer.

"Words. Empty words." He shoved Kael again. Enoch closed his eyes. The orb pulsed once, twice. Suddenly, the ground beneath the boys trembled not breaking, not harming, just a deep vibration like the heartbeat of the earth. Their laughter caught in their throats. Fear flickered across their faces. Kael stood tall, no longer shaking. The bully stepped back, uncertain. Enoch opened his eyes. The light dimmed. He looked at Kael. "You see? Violence would have satisfied you for a moment. "But this" he gestured to the silence, to the bullies retreating with uneasy glances, "this change how they see you. Not as prey. Not as equal. But as someone they cannot break."

Kael's breath came fast, chest rising with a new weight. He looked at the older man with awe. "Then kindness… is power?" Enoch's lips curved faintly, almost a smile. "Kindness is restraint. Restraint is power. And power… must never be wasted on proving what is already true."

Confused by what had just happened, the boys became dismissive of Kael and simply walked away. Kael remained, still trembling but taller than before. Enoch placed the orb back into his robe. Quietly, so only Kael could hear, he said: "Remember, sir, the strongest strike you will ever make is the one you choose not to." The path emptied.

The boys were gone. Kael still stood, chest lifted, eyes alight with something new. Enoch drew a long breath and slipped the orb back into his palm. Its light dimmed as his fingers curled around it. But just before his hand closed, he froze. Beside the orb, resting quietly against his skin, was another grain of wheat. Enoch stared. His heart tightened. He had taken only one. Yet now there are two. He closed his hand slowly, reverently. Each trial, each truth shared… is it lifting the burden? Returning what I lost? The wind stirred, carrying the scent of the sea and something sweeter like harvest.

The storm realm was not done with him. A deeper trial awaited. Kael looked up at him, voice small but hopeful. "Are you going home now?" Enoch said nothing. He only turned his eyes to the horizon. I can never go home, he thought.

As the drizzle gave way to a pale horizon, Kael lingered beside Enoch, his eyes still wide with the weight of new lessons. He hesitated, then tugged at Enoch's sleeve. "You should come with me," he said softly. "My mother will want to thank you." There was no demand in the boy's tone, only quiet hope. Enoch almost refused, his heart still raw, his steps bound to exile, but the invitation carried a warmth he could not turn from. And so, he followed Kael down the narrow path, toward a modest home where a fire still burned and a woman named Mira waited, unaware that her life and his were about to intertwine.

Chapter Three–Closing Sequence

The fire in Mira's small home burned low, shadows stretching long against the walls. Enoch sat across from her, speaking little, intent on giving her space. "You need no offering for gratitude," he said gently. "Your strength is already enough." But Mira shook her head. Her eyes, tired yet luminous, lingered on him. "I have given myself too many for survival. But never for this." She stepped closer, voice trembling. "You stood for me. You looked at me without shame. I cannot let you leave as though you were no one."

Enoch turned his gaze away, orb heavy in his palm. "You do not owe me this." "This is not debt," she said firmly. "This is desire. My own." For a long time, he resisted, the weight of his exile pressing hard. Yet her insistence was not desperation.

It was a discovery, the awakening of a woman who had never known what it was to want without being used. Enoch yielded. And in yielding, for the first time in countless ages, he felt the past loosen its grip.

There were no visions of feasts or rejections, no flashbacks of what was lost. Only the warmth of another body, the immediacy of touch, and a moment that belonged entirely to the present. For a while, Enoch was not in exile. He was simply a man.

But at dawn, when he rose quietly and checked the orb, his breath caught. The glow was faint, its constellations dim. And where there had been two grains of wheat, there were now none. He stared, heart pounding. "What does this mean?" The chamber grew heavy, the air was thick. The Custodian's voice moved like a current through his mind, neither harsh nor kind: "With knowledge comes power. And with power, intent must be mindful. You did not intend a covenant, yet a covenant was made. For when you yielded without transaction, you entered freely. Desire sealed what barter never could." Enoch sank to his knees, the orb clutched tight. He was no longer burdened by rejection, yet something had been stripped from him, a reminder that even freedom demanded cost. He looked toward Mira, sleeping softly, her face untroubled for the first time in years. "I must walk carefully," he whispered. "Even love can bind as chains."

Chapter Four–The Trial of Reciprocity

The morning air clung damply to the cliffs. Enoch rose before dawn, the orb dull in his palm, its light no more than a whisper. He had slept little. The second grain of wheat was gone, his covenant with Mira still pressing heavily on his chest. He told himself it was time to walk on. Time to follow the call of the horizon. He gathered his robe about him and moved quietly through the narrow paths, hoping to slip away unnoticed. The wind carried the salt of the sea and the faint echo of the village behind him.

"Master!" The voice startled him. He turned. Kael was coming down the path, arms full of reeds and baskets from the morning's errands, a smile on his face that made Enoch's chest tighten. "You're up early," the boy said breathlessly. "I thought we could go to the market today. You promised to show me more." Enoch's jaw tightened. The boy's eagerness was heavier than the sea. He turned back toward the horizon, his steps measured, silent. "Wait," Kael's voice cracked, small and raw. "You weren't just going to leave… were you?" Enoch stopped. His shoulders rose and fell with a long breath. He did not turn. For a moment, the silence was cruel. Then, reluctantly, he faced the boy. "I will return," he said at last, his voice low but steady. "Tell your mother I said so." Kael's eyes searched his, doubtful yet clinging to the words. He nodded and, with trembling hands, reached into his tunic. From beneath the fabric, he drew out a pendant, simple but worn smooth by years of touch. Its surface was etched with faded lines, almost gone, yet Kael held it as though it were gold. "This is the most valuable thing I have," the boy said, pressing it into Enoch's hand. "Take it. Use it to barter wherever you go. But bring it back. Because I trust you." Enoch's throat tightened. The pendant was light, yet it weighed on him heavily than the orb itself. He closed his hand around it, the orb and the gift together, and gave a small nod. "I will bring it back."

The path bent away from the cliffs and carried him toward the valley. Days passed as he wandered, following the faint pull of the orb. At last, he reached a city, vast, alive, bursting with markets and voices. Here, Enoch thrived. He spoke in tongues that the traders did not know but soon understood. He healed the sick with herbs and methods beyond their reach. He sketched devices in the sand, pumps, pulleys, and mechanisms that made labor lighter. His wisdom turned to coin, and coin to comfort. Robes of fine cloth were draped upon him, tables heavy with food set before him. He was courted by merchants and rulers alike. Yet always, when he returned to his chamber, the pendant lay in his hand. Its simple lines seemed to glow against the wealth that surrounded him. One evening, as the city prepared a feast in his honor, Enoch sat alone.

He opened his hand. The orb glowed faintly, constellations shifting like restless eyes. A voice, soft but absolute, moved within him: "Prosperity is not proof of purpose. Reciprocity demands return. What you hold that is not yours must go back." Enoch closed his eyes. The feast awaited, the city's riches his for the taking. But Kael's face rose in his mind, hopeful, trembling, trusting. He stood. At the city gates, he looked back once more. Lights glimmered in the streets, laughter rising like music. His robe was heavy with coin, his belt weighed down by wealth he had never sought but easily won. "I could build a kingdom here," he whispered. "But what is a kingdom if it is built on the foundation of a broken covenant?"

He turned from the lights and walked into the dark. The road stretched toward the cliffs once more, toward Kael and Mira. When he opened his hand, the pendant lay beside the orb, and nestled against it, a third grain of wheat. Enoch walked into the dark, the city fading behind him. The pendant warmed in his hand, the grain of wheat glowing beside it.

Things borrowed must be returned. Not diminished but restored. To fail is not forgetfulness, but theft against the soul itself. The city had offered him riches, but the boy had offered him trust. And trust was weightier than gold. What is borrowed must be given back. What is trusted must be made whole. For a man is not measured by what he takes, but by what he restores. The orb pulsed faintly, as if it too had heard the law whispered by the Custodian: Return all things you borrow. Return them not lessened, but greater than before. For this is the law that binds the living and the lost. Enoch closed his hand. He carried not just wealth, but restoration. And with it, he carried the right to walk forward.

Chapter Five–The Trial of Covenant / Intent

The city did not let Enoch leave empty-handed. His wisdom had filled their markets with new tools, healed their sick, and settled disputes that once tore neighbors apart. When he chose to depart, they honored him with horses, coins, and supplies enough to last many roads. At his side rode a century, a young soldier who had once known only orders and obedience. Under Enoch's teaching, he had grown sharper, braver, steadier. If Kael had been Enoch's shadow of innocence, the century was his shadow of strength.

Together, they set out toward the cliffs and the promise of return. For days, they traveled through valleys and plains, until they came upon a caravan of weary travelers, merchants and families with wagons heavy and faces drawn from the road. Among them walked a young woman, her eyes bright even through dust and hunger. The century noticed her instantly. He avoided her gaze, but Enoch saw the tremor in his composure. That night by the fire, the century spoke, his voice low. "I have faced battle without trembling. But in her presence, I am undone. I have nothing to offer her, no wealth, no name." Enoch studied him a long while, then placed the orb in his hand. It flared once, then dimmed, inert to all but its master. "You do not need what you do not have," Enoch said. "You have bravery. And bravery is wealth to the weary. It has value to her and to this caravan. That is your inheritance and authentic gift." The next day, the century walked at the front of the caravan. His voice carried steady commands, his eyes watched the horizon.

When raiders appeared in the distance, he did not falter. He lifted a staff and rallied the guards with courage that spread like fire. The caravan held their ground, and the danger passed. That night, the young woman smiled at him, not as one may pity, but as one respects. By dawn, Enoch knew it was time. He pressed a purse of coins and provisions into the century's hand. "You are no longer a follower," he said. "You are a leader now. This caravan is yours." The century bowed deeply. "You have given me more than coin. You have given me a name." Enoch turned away, leading only his horses into the open road. His wealth was lighter, yet his spirit heavier with the weight of covenant. The pendant pressed against his chest. The wheat glimmered faintly in his palm. But ahead, the horizon darkened.

Clouds rolled heavily, swallowing the sky. Thunder cracked across the cliffs, and rain struck his face like cold fire. The road would not yield easily. It would demand patience.

Chapter Six–The Trial of Patience

The sky closed like a fist. Wind tore at Enoch's robe, rain striking in hard, slanted lines. The orb in his palm dimmed to a coal, its constellations muffled as if even light had to bow before the storm. He pressed onward until the path vanished under sheets of water and the horses balked, whites of their eyes flashing. Enoch laid a steady hand on each muzzle, breathing slowly until their panic settled into shivers. The cliffs offered a jagged seam in the rock, no comfort, only shelter.
They squeezed inside, rain drumming the stone like a thousand fists. Cold ate at his bones. Hunger arrived without drama, just a quiet vacancy widening under his ribs.

He wrapped the horses with his cloak, leaving his shoulders to the wind that found its way through the cracks. Outside, the world roared. Inside, time stretched thin. Minutes lengthened into hours, and hours into something shapeless. The storm was a mouth that chewed the edges of thought.

Enoch closed his eyes and found himself drifting toward memory Mira's warm, steady breath at dawn; Kael's bright eyes, the trembling courage that lifted his chin; the century's new name spoken over a fire. Each memory pulled at him like harbor lights. Why walk at all? The ache suggested. Stay where warmth already knows your name.

The horses stamped, and the cave answered with a low, patient echo. Enoch drew the orb to his chest. The pulse within it matched his own, faint but faithful. He let the storm be a storm. He did not curse it. He did not bargain with it. He listened first to the wind, then to the rain, then to the smaller sounds beneath both: the slow drip from a stalactite, the soft rasp of a horse's breath, the near-silent thread of his own heartbeat weaving through the noise. Time warped there, the way it does near great weights.

He felt the hours pull long and thin, the way a river slows around a bend. Waiting became its own gravity, asking him not to conquer the storm but to survive its measure. The voice of the Custodian moved through the stone, warm and unhurried: "Patience is not waiting for stillness. Patience is still within the storm. Learn to smile during the chaos, so when your memory relives it, it does not traumatize you twice." Enoch exhaled. He let a small, improbable smile find him in the dark. Not defiance acceptance. The cave did not warm. The wind did not quiet. But something in him unclenched, and the night passed through him instead of lodging inside. Near dawn, the rain thinned. The roar eased to a hush. The world returned in pieces first the pale seam of horizon, then the slick shine of the path, then the heavy, grateful quiet that follows endurance. Enoch stepped out with the horses. The air smelled washed and newborn. He opened his hand. The orb brightened clean, awake. Nestled beside it lay a single grain of wheat, bright as a small sun. He closed his fingers around the gifts and looked to the road that bent back toward the cliffs. "Even storms must pass," he said, and this time the smile was easier. He walked.

Chapter Seven–The Trial of Balance

The dawn was soft when Enoch finally returned to the cliffs. The sea murmured below, and the small home stood as he remembered, though its edges were more weathered by time. Inside, Kael slept, no longer the boy who had pressed the pendant into his hand but a youth grown tall and sturdy, shoulders broadened by labor, face tempered by years.

Enoch knelt beside him and placed the pendant back into his palm before he stirred. Kael's fingers curled instinctively, as if even in sleep he still trusted the promise. Enoch lingered there, hand resting briefly over the boy, then rose to wait for him to wake. The house bore signs of life. Food prepared recently, garments folded neatly, a faint scent of herbs clinging to the air.

Mira was not inside, but her presence was. Then came the sound muffled at first, then clearer. Weeping. Enoch stepped outside and saw her, coming up the path with a basket against her hip, her shoulders bent. Her tears fell unchecked, her face drawn with exhaustion.

But when she lifted her head and saw him standing there, her cry caught in her throat. She dropped the basket. "Enoch…" He held the reins of two horses, packs laden with coin and cloth, provisions greater than anything she had ever laid eyes on. Her weeping stopped. Her eyes widened, joy overtaking sorrow like a river bursting its banks. She rushed forward, laughter replacing tears. "You came back! And with more than I could have dreamed!" Whatever had troubled her vanished in the flood of relief. Her laughter stirred Kael from his bed. He stumbled outside, the pendant still in hand, blinking into the morning light. When he saw Enoch standing there, alive, his breath caught. "You kept your promise," he whispered. The three of them embraced, Mira's arms tight around them both.

For the first time in years, their home rang with celebration. That night became a feast. Neighbors came, drawn by the sound of laughter and music. Fires burned brightly, bread was shared, and wine poured. Kael glowed in the light, eyes full of wonder, questions spilling from his lips as Enoch told stories of cities, caravans, storms, and patience. Mira sat close, her hand brushing Enoch's as she smiled at the wealth spread before them. The celebration stretched long into the night. But when the fires dimmed and the laughter grew softer, Enoch felt the imbalance settle.

Mira looked at him as if waiting for something unspoken, something permanent. He felt the weight of it and knew why. He had thought wealth would free her; that abundance would erase the need for her old survival. But he had been gone, and they had only shared a single night before his departure.

To Mira, he had never spoken a covenant aloud. The message had come through Kael, not from his own lips. And she, who had known lies too many times before, had never truly believed his return was bound by promise. To her, tonight was joy. But to him, it was a reckoning. The celebration closed with song, but Enoch's eyes lingered on the fire's last embers.
Balance, he realized, was not measured in coin or return.
It was in truth spoken, and truth withheld.

Chapter Eight–The Trial of Release

The house was quiet after the feast. The embers glowed low, the air heavy with wine and laughter, now faded. Enoch sat across from Mira, the silence between them louder than the songs had been. At last, he spoke. "Can I stay?" Her eyes searched his face.

She did not answer quickly, and in her pause, he filled the silence with his own confession. "When I left, I believed that if I returned with wealth, you would no longer have to endure the life you had before. I thought you would see me as covenant, as permanence. But I never spoke such a vow with my own lips. That was my failing. You did nothing wrong." Mira's gaze softened, but she said nothing still.

Enoch drew a long breath. "Your survival was strength. I mistook my own longing for a promise you never received." Something loosened in him as he spoke. A revelation rose with it: everything on earth is borrowed. Wealth, bonds, even time itself. What he had thought of as loss had never been his to keep. Every bond, every gift, every trial had been a catalyst, placed in his hands for a season, to be returned greater than it was given. He looked to Mira. "I have not lost. I have inherited. Each trial, each bond, a seed to create what is needed in this time fiber, something that can outlive me in this realm."

At last, she reached across the table, her hand brushing his. "You may stay," she said softly. "But not as husband. I will not bind a covenant where it was never spoken. Still," her voice caught, then steadied, "your place is here, if you choose it." Enoch bowed his head. It was enough. The orb brightened at his side, and when he opened his palm, another grain of wheat lay there, shining with quiet promise. But outside, in the dark beyond the cliffs, shadows stirred. Word had spread of his return.

The boys who had once mocked Kael were no longer boys. They had grown into men hardened by legions, their cruelty sharpened into violence. Whispers told of their rise, of power gathered into their hands. Enoch stood at the threshold, the weight of revelation and the weight of inevitability pressing equally against him. Balance was fleeting. Storms gathered still. "All things are borrowed," he whispered to himself. "But if I return them greater, they will live beyond me." And though laughter still lingered in the house behind him, the horizon ahead promised a trial darker than any storm.

www.ingramcontent.com/pod-product-compliance
Lightning Source LLC
LaVergne TN
LVHW040222110826
845146LV00005B/1376

* 9 7 9 8 9 9 3 3 0 0 1 1 5 *